W9-AAG-979

by J. Powell

illustrated by
Paul Savage

Librarian Reviewer
Joanne Bongaarts
Educational Consultant
MS in Library Media Education, Minnesota State University, Mankato, MN
Teacher and Media Specialist with Edina Public Schools, MN, 1993–2000

Reading Consultant
Elizabeth Stedem
Educator/Consultant, Colorado Springs, CO
MA in Elementary Education, University of Denver, CO

 **STONE ARCH BOOKS**
Minneapolis   San Diego

First published in the United States in 2006
by Stone Arch Books,
151 Good Counsel Drive, P.O. Box 669,
Mankato, Minnesota 56002.
www.stonearchbooks.com

Originally published in Great Britain in 2004
by Badger Publishing Ltd.

Original work copyright © 2005 Badger Publishing Ltd
Text copyright © 2005 Jillian Powell

All rights reserved. No part of this publication may be reproduced
in whole or in part, or stored in a retrieval system, or transmitted in any
form or by any means, electronic, mechanical, photocopying, recording,
or otherwise, without written permission of the publisher.

Library of Congress Cataloging-in-Publication Data
Powell, Jillian.
    Code Breakers / by J. Powell; illustrated by Paul Savage.
    p. cm.
    "Keystone Books."
    Summary: Brad, Conor, and Scott are bored until they find a suitcase
containing a cell phone number that leads them on an adventure. Following
one clue after another, they find a treasure in a cave—but can they find their
way out again?
    ISBN-13: 978-1-59889-010-5 (hardcover)
    ISBN-10: 1-59889-010-7 (hardcover)
    [1. Ciphers—Fiction. 2. Adventure and adventurers—Fiction.]
I. Savage, Paul, 1971– ill. II. Title.
PZ7.P87755Cod 2006
[Fic]—dc22   2005026337

1 2 3 4 5 6 11 10 09 08 07 06

Printed in the United States of America

TABLE OF CONTENTS

Chapter 1

A STRANGE FIND

"Stop doing that!" Brad said to his friend Conor. "You're bothering me!"

Conor was kicking a can around the park.

"We could go down to the arcade," Scott said.

"You got any money?" Brad asked him.

Conor stopped kicking the can.
"What's that over there?" he asked.

The boys ran over to a bench.
Someone had left an old briefcase there.

"Open it up," Brad said. "It might be
stuffed with money!"

"Don't!" exclaimed Conor. "It might be a bomb or something."

His friends made chicken noises.

Brad opened the case, and they all looked inside.

"That's weird," said Brad.

He took out a ball of string, a map, a postcard, and a key.

"What's that say?" Scott asked. There were numbers on the postcard.

"It's a cell phone number," Brad told him.

Brad took out his cell phone.

"What are you doing?" Conor asked. "This could be a trap."

"Yeah! Like this was a bomb!" Scott threw the ball of string into the bushes.

"What are you waiting for? Call the number!" Scott said to Brad.

"There might be a reward or something," Scott added.

"Or something like our heads blown off," Conor said.

Brad ignored Conor and dialed the number.

Chapter 2

"What do you hear?" Scott asked.

Brad shook his head. "It's a voice mail," he said. "But it's just repeating a number and a letter."

"Let me hear," Scott said, taking the phone from Brad.

"Got a pen?" Scott asked. "I know what this is. It's coordinates on that map we found."

Scott wrote the coordinates down.

"Now hand me the map," Scott said to Conor.

"Okay. I did this in geography class," Scott said. "Looks like we're at 3-C on the map, right? What were those coordinates again?"

"5-F," Brad told him.

"So we go down two to 5, and then over three to F," Scott explained.

Brad and Conor looked blank.

"That's it!" Scott pointed at the map. "That's the place."

"Where is it?" Brad asked. "I mean, where is it from here?"

"Not that far," Scott said. "We could walk it, easy."

"I wonder what all this means," Brad said. "I mean, the cell phone, the map . . . it's like a code or something."

"A trap, you mean. And we're falling right into it," Conor added.

"It's better than kicking a can around all day," Brad told him.

"Do you think we should take this stuff with us?" Scott asked.

"Leave the case. Just bring the key and what we found inside," Brad said.

Scott took the map, and the others followed him.

* * *

"According to this map, it's got to be over there somewhere," Scott explained to them.

"Well, we hardly needed the map,"
Conor said. "Look!"

Conor was pointing at a big circle
on the ground with an X in its center.

"That's a landing pad," Scott said.

The others could hardly hear him. A
helicopter was heading toward them.

Chapter 3

"It's going to land! Quick! Hide!"
Brad shouted.

The helicopter was right above
them. They ran toward some bushes
and hid.

"I told you it was a trap!" Conor
exclaimed. "They're probably drug
dealers or something, and we —"

"Quiet!" Brad cut him off.

"Look!" he added. "They're not landing. They dropped something."

"I told you — drugs!" Conor said.

"One way to find out," Scott said.

They watched until the helicopter flew out of sight. When it was safe, Brad went and picked up the box.

"It feels warm," Brad said. "Wonder what's inside?" Brad opened it. They all looked with amazement. There were three steaming hot dogs inside.

"Cool!" Scott said. "I'm starving."

"Are you crazy?" Conor asked. "They could be poisoned!"

"Smells great!" Scott said. He grabbed one of the hot dogs. "I wonder if there's any ketchup. I like ketchup on mine."

Scott opened the bun.

"What's that?" Brad asked, pointing at the bun in Scott's hand.

Scott was about to take a bite. He stopped halfway.

"There's some sort of stamp on the bun. Letters or something," said Scott.

"Not more map coordinates?" Brad asked.

"Don't think so," Scott replied.

"Let me see." Conor took a look.

"I know what that is," Conor said. "It's a Dewey number."

"A what?" Scott asked.

"You know, in the library, all books have a Dewey Decimal number. That's how you find them."

"Okay, so this hot dog is really a book?" Brad asked.

This was getting crazier all the time.

"No. Don't you see? It's another code," Conor said. "And it looks like our next stop is the library."

Chapter 4

A HOLE CLUE

The next day, the boys went straight to the library. Conor had written the Dewey number on the postcard.

"Okay, so we're looking for these numbers," he told the others. "Every book has a Dewey number."

"It's got to be over here," Brad said. "Okay! Got it!"

Brad pulled a book from a shelf.

"*Caves and Caving*," Brad read.

"So what do we do now?" Scott asked. "I can't read all that!" The book was very thick.

"Look inside," Conor said.

Brad started looking through the book. "Looks really boring," he said. "You sure this is the right one?"

"What was that?" Conor asked. "Go back a page. Look! There's a hole punched in the page."

"Vandals!" Scott exclaimed. "I once took a book out, and someone had written all over —"

"No, don't you see?" Brad said. "That's it! What does it say on that page, Conor?"

"It's just about this boring old cave," Conor said. "You still got the map?"

Brad took out the map.

"Cook's Cave. Can you see anything called that?" asked Conor.

"Yeah. It's there, look." Scott pointed at the map. "It's by the beach."

"Okay, what are we waiting for?" Brad asked. "Better pick up a flashlight on the way."

It was a long walk to the beach, but they found the cave easily.

"It's dark in there," Conor said. He shined the beam.

"Yeah, we know. It's a trap, right?" Brad said with a grin.

The cave was a maze of dark, gloomy tunnels. It did feel like a trap.

"We can't go any farther," Conor said. "There's water in here."

"Yes, we can," Brad said. "Look. There's a boat!"

They climbed inside.

"Start paddling!" Scott said. "We can't give up now!"

Chapter 5

THE KEY FITS

They paddled the boat deeper into the cave.

"There's got to be something in here," Brad said. "The codes all lead here. Right?"

"These tunnels all look alike," Scott said. "Anyone remember if we've been down this passage before?"

"Yeah. I remember that big rock," Conor said.

"Wait!" Brad shouted. "Give me the flashlight, Scott."

Brad shined the flashlight into a corner of the cave.

"Bingo!" he said. "Look, over there!"

"Looks like the briefcase we found in the park," Scott said. "Can't be, can it?"

"It's got a lock on it," Brad said. "The key — remember!"

Brad tried the lock. There was a loud click, and the case opened.

"Wow!" the boys exclaimed in amazement. The case was full of bundles of money.

"We're rich!" Brad shouted. He waved a bundle in the air.

"It could be fake or stolen," Conor said. "We should get out of here."

"Well, we're not going without this!" Brad said.

Brad and Scott pulled the case into the boat.

"Okay. Let's get out of here," Brad said.

"Yeah, but which way?" Scott asked.

"Try that way," Brad said.

* * *

Some time later, Conor saw the big
rock again.

"I knew it," he said. "We're going
around in circles. We're never going to
get out of here!"

"Hey, the string!" Brad said. "I
played this computer game once. You
had to get out of this maze, and you
used string to mark where you'd been.
That way you don't . . ."

His voice trailed off. Scott had
thrown the string into the bushes. It
was probably still there.

Chapter 6

THE FINAL CODE

"That's it," Conor said. "We're trapped. One day someone will find three skeletons with a lot of money."

"We're doomed!" added Brad.

"We could try shouting," Scott said. "There may be someone on the beach."

"Help! Help!" Their voices echoed around the cave.

Suddenly, there was a blaze of lights, and a voice said, "You are on this week's episode of *Code Breakers!*"

"We've been following you with our hidden cameras," the voice continued. "You have almost won the top prize."

"But you have to get the case out of the cave to win the money!" added the voice. "There is one more code to solve and just 60 seconds left!"

The countdown began.

"60, 59 . . ."

"It's got to be here somewhere, guys!" Conor shouted.

"50, 49, 48 . . ."

"Wait! I see something!" Conor pointed at some marks on the wall.

"It's just a bunch of dots and stuff," Scott said.

"Yeah, but if I'm right, that's Morse code," Conor said. "We learned Morse code in scouts, years ago."

"20, 19, 18 . . ."

"Well?" Brad and Scott looked like they were going to burst.

Conor wrote something with his finger on his palm.

"16, 15 . . ."

"That dot is an E," he said slowly.

"And I think that may be an X . . .
Let's see. E-X . . ."

His face lit up.

"Row like crazy, guys!" he told them.
"That code says EXIT!"

ABOUT THE AUTHOR

Jillian Powell started writing when she was very young. She loved having a giant pad of paper and some pens or crayons in front of her. She made up newspaper stories about jewel thieves and spies. Jillian's parents still have her early stories, complete with crayon illustrations!

ABOUT THE ILLUSTRATOR

Paul Savage works in a design studio, drawing pictures for advertising. He says illustrating books is "the best job." He's always been interested in illustrating books, and he loves reading. Paul also enjoys playing sports and running.

He lives in England with his wife and daughter, Amelia.

caving (KAYV-ing)—the sport of exploring caves

coordinates (koh-OR-duh-nits)—a set of numbers or letters that show the position on a map

Dewey Decimal number (DOO-ee DESS-uh-muhl NUHM-bur)—a number printed on a book that tells the book's location in a library

geography (jee-OG-ruh-fee)—the study of Earth, especially its physical features, such as mountains, caves, and rivers

Morse code (MORSS KODE)—a way of signaling that uses a pattern of dots and dashes

vandal (VAN-duhl)—someone who damages or destroys other people's property

DISCUSSION QUESTIONS

1. When the boys first find the case, Scott throws the ball of string into the bushes. How does this action later affect the boys?

2. What do you think would have happened at the end of the story if Conor didn't know Morse code?

3. Scott and Brad are daring, while Conor acts more carefully. How do each of the boys' personalities help the group?

WRITING PROMPTS

1. When the boys first find the briefcase, Conor tells them to leave it alone. He's afraid it could be a bomb or a trap. Write what you would do if you found an old case on a park bench. Would you open it or leave it alone? Why?

2. If you were with the boys as they followed the clues, would you have been afraid? Explain why you would or wouldn't be afraid?

3. What would you do if you found a lot of money? Would you look for its owner or keep it? Explain.

ALSO BY J. POWELL

5010 Calling
1-59889-012-3

Beta lives in the year 5010, and many things are different about his world. What happens when he taps into the mind of Zac, who lives in 2000? What does he learn about the past? And what does Zac learn about the future?

Webcam Scam
1-59889-011-5

Carl's family is thrilled when they are chosen for a reality Web show. Carl is not sure. When it seems that there is more to it than meets the eye, Carl has to act.

OTHER BOOKS IN THIS SET

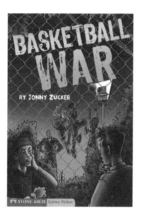

Basketball War
by Jonny Zucker
1-59889-009-3

*Jim and Ali are determined
to beat the Langham Jets
in the upcoming basketball
championship. But the boys
learn that there's something
strange about their rivals'
new coach.*

Nervous
by Tony Norman
1-59889-018-2

*It's time for the Dream Stars
competition. The cool kids
think their band Elite is a
sure win. But what happens
when a couple of nerds decide
to start up their own band
called Nervous?*

INTERNET SITES

Do you want to know more about subjects related to this book? Or are you interested in learning about other topics? Then check out FactHound, a fun, easy way to find Internet sites.

Our investigative staff has already sniffed out great sites for you!

Here's how to use FactHound:

1. Visit *www.facthound.com*

2. Select your grade level.

3. To learn more about subjects related to this book, type in the book's ISBN number: **1598890107**.

4. Click the **Fetch It** button.

FactHound will fetch the best Internet sites for you!